For Melanie Kroupa,
who really needs one!

A Red Fox Book

Published by Random House Children's Books
20 Vauxhall Bridge Road, London SW1V 2SA

A division of Random House UK Ltd
London Melbourne Sydney Auckland
Johannesburg and agencies throughout the world

Copyright © 1993 Marc Brown

3 5 7 9 10 8 6 4 2

First published in the United States of America by
Little, Brown & Company and simultaneously in Canada by
Little, Brown & Company (Canada) Ltd 1993

First published in Great Britain by Red Fox 1997

Printed in Hong Kong

RANDOM HOUSE UK Limited Reg. No. 954009

ISBN 0 09 921912 3

It was Arthur's last day of school.
Mr Ratburn gave the class a surprise spelling test.
All the other classes were having parties.
"Finally, the moment you've all been waiting for,"
said Mr Ratburn. "Reports and . . .

". . . school's out!"

Everyone cheered.

"I can't wait for baseball practice to start," said Francine.

"I'm taking a college computer course," the Brain announced.

"I'll really miss you at Camp Meadowcroak this year, Arthur," Buster said.

"I wish I didn't have to go on holiday with my family," said Arthur. "There'll be nothing to do and no one to do it with."

"You'll have D.W.," Buster said, smiling. "For a whole week."

"Don't remind me," said Arthur.

Arthur's family spent that night packing.

"I wish I could take my doll's house," said D.W.

"I wish Buster could come," said Arthur.

"This is a *family* holiday," said Mother.

"All we need for fun is each other," said Father.

"Let's take my swing set," said D.W. "We can all use that."

"Well, we're all packed," Father said the next morning.
"Where's Arthur?"
"He's on the phone to Buster," said Mother.
"For the hundredth time," D.W. added.
"Before we leave," said Father, "does anyone need
to use the bathroom?"
"This is your last chance," said Mother.
"Don't look at me!" said D.W.

"On our way at last." Mother smiled. "A whole week of no cooking!"

"And no dishes," said Father.

"A whole week without my best friend in the whole wide world," moaned Arthur.

"Once you're at the beach, you'll feel better," Father said.

"Are we there yet?" asked D.W. "I need to go to the bathroom."

Arthur spent the rest of the trip thinking about how much fun Buster must be having at camp.

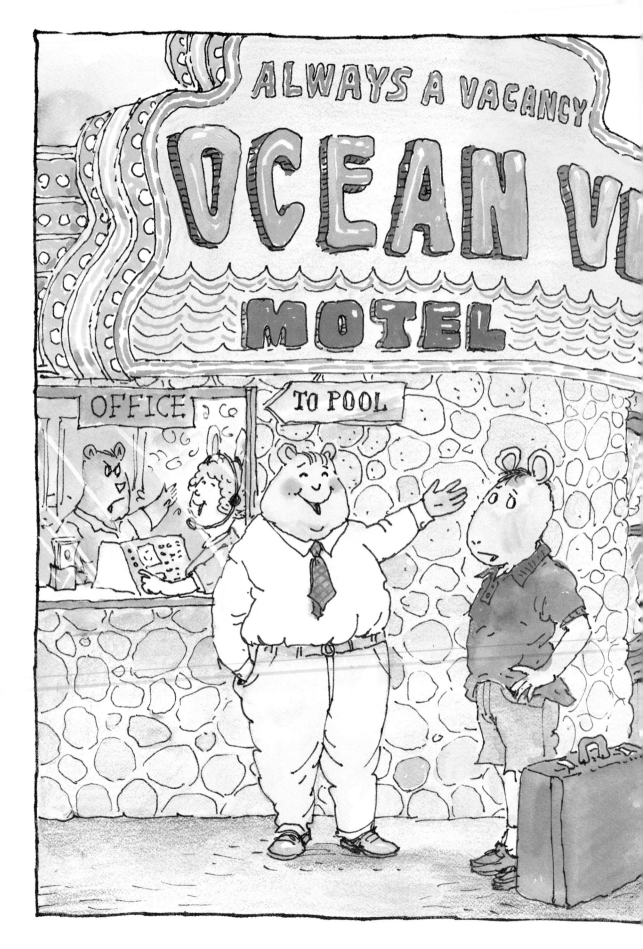

"We're here!" said Mother.

"Welcome to Ocean View," said the manager.

"Where's the ocean?" asked Father.

"Just over the road behind that shopping centre."
The manager pointed. "But there's a pool right here."

"Well, I think I'll go swimming," said Arthur.

"Me, too," said D.W. "Wait for me!"

"Let's see our room first," said Mother.

"You mean we all have to stay in this puny little room?" asked D.W.

"Don't worry," said Mother. "We'll only be sleeping here."

"If you want to swim," said Arthur, "hurry up and get your swimsuit on."

"We've got the whole pool to ourselves," said Arthur.
"It's a good thing, too," said D.W. "Our bathtub is
bigger than this!"

That night at dinner, everyone ordered lobster.
"Buster loves lobster!" said Arthur.
"*This* is lobster?" said D.W. "I want a hot dog."

"Can we go to the beach tomorrow?" Arthur asked. "Good idea!" said Father. "I'm sure the rain will have stopped by then."

"No beach today!" D.W. announced the next morning.

"I had a dream about Buster," said Arthur.

"Why don't you write him a postcard?" Mother suggested.

"Why don't we all write postcards?" said Father.

"But what shall we write about?" said D.W. "We haven't done anything yet!"

"What do we do now?" said D.W. "This holiday is a disaster."

"At camp there's always something fun to do," thought Arthur. "Even on rainy days."

"That's it!" he said. "I'm taking us all on a day trip."

"I've never heard of a *cow* festival," D.W. said. "But at least it's more fun than our motel room."

"Say 'cheese'," said Father.

"Let's hurry up or we'll miss the milking contest," said Arthur.

For the next few days, it rained and rained, but Arthur didn't mind. He was too busy planning new places to go to. He forgot all about missing Buster.

On Wednesday, they went to Gatorville.
"At least the alligators get to swim," said D.W.

Thursday was busy, too. After touring Flo's Fudge Factory, they all went on Jimmy's Jungle Cruise.

"I never realized there were so many fun things to do in the rain," said Father.

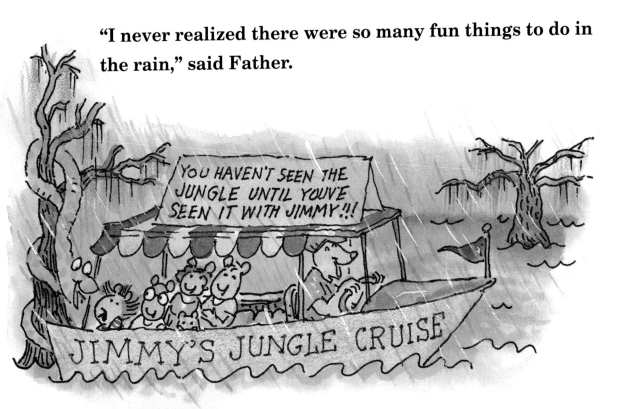

"I want to plan a day trip, too," said D.W. "To the movies."

But when they got there, D.W. was too scared to watch.
"I thought it was a movie about fish," she whispered.

Finally, on Friday, their last day, the sun came out.

"What a day!" said Father.

"Just glorious!" said Mother.

Even D.W. was having fun.

No one wanted to leave, but the next day, they packed up
and headed home.

"We're almost there," said Mother.

"Phew!" said D.W. "I really need to go to the bathroom."

"Oh, boy," said Arthur, "I can't wait to see Buster."

As soon as they got home, the doorbell rang.
It was Buster.

"Camp was fun, but I missed you," he said to Arthur.

"How was your holiday? How did you and D.W. get
along?"

"Great!" said Arthur. "Take a look."

"Wow!" said Buster. "You really did have a great time."